In the Diner

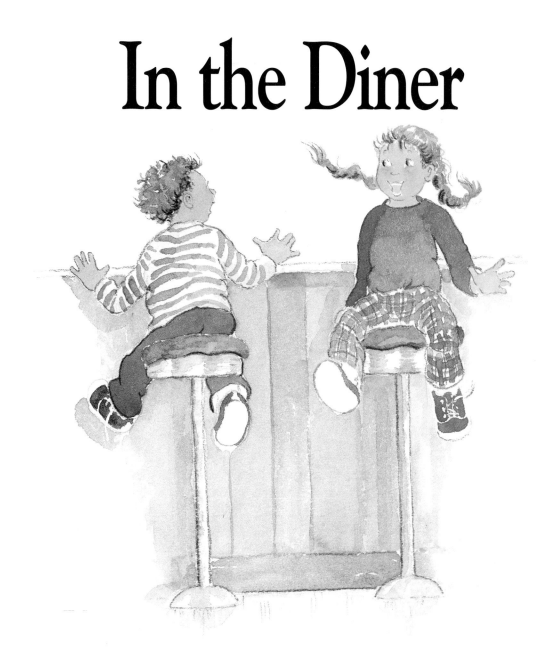

Written by Christine Loomis
Illustrated by Nancy Poydar

NEW YORK TORONTO LONDON AUCKLAND SYDNEY

Library of Congress Catalog Card Number: 93-84594

Library of Congress Cataloging-in-Publication Data

Loomis, Christine, September, 1993
In the Diner / by Christine Loomis; illustrated by Nancy Poydar.
p.cm. — (Scholastic My First Library)
Summary: Neighborhood people are introduced and the
sights and sounds of a day in a diner are told in pictures and verse.

ISBN 0-590-49487-2   ISBN 0-590-29290-0 (meets NASTA specifications)

3 4 5 6 7 8 9 10   09   08 07 06 05 04

Printed in the U.S.A.
First Scholastic printing, September 1993.

For Kira,
whose unique approach
to food and
well-developed sense of
humor make her a fascinating
dining companion.
— C.L.

For elementary
school teachers, especially my
former colleagues.
— N.P.

JOE'S DINER

In the diner ...

5

Waiters hurry.

Busboys scurry.

Bacon sizzles.
Syrup drizzles.

Coffee brews.
Beef stews.

Bagels toast.
Turkeys roast.

Soap bubbles.
Dough doubles.

Baker stirs.
Cat purrs.

12

Cook flips.
Scale tips.

Cake bakes.

Cat wakes.

Burgers broil.
Sauces boil.

Fish grills.
Gravy spills.

17

Hostess greets.

Crowd eats.

Girl hides.

Dog guides.

Platters clatter.
People chatter.

Stool twirls.

Chocolate swirls!

Ice cream freezes.
Someone sneezes.

Boy slurps.
Baby burps.

Waiters stack.
Cups crack.

Saucers clunk.
Washers dunk.

People pay.
It's a day

... in the diner.